A Note to Parents and Caregivers:

Read-it! Readers are for children who are just starting on the amazing road to reading. These beautiful books support both the acquisition of reading skills and the love of books.

The RED LEVEL presents familiar topics using common words and repeating sentence patterns.

The BLUE LEVEL presents new ideas using a larger vocabulary and varied sentence structure.

The YELLOW LEVEL presents more challenging ideas, a broad vocabulary, and wide variety in sentence structure.

The GREEN LEVEL presents more complex ideas, an extended vocabulary range, and expanded language structures.

When sharing a book with your child, read in short stretches, pausing often to talk about the pictures. Have your child turn the pages and point to the pictures and familiar words. Be sure to reread favorite stories or parts of stories.

There is no right or wrong way to share books with children. Find time to read with your child, and pass on the legacy of literacy.

Adria F. Klein, Ph.D.
Professor Emeritus
California State University
San Bernardino, California

Managing Editor: Bob Temple
Creative Director: Terri Foley
Editor: Peggy Henrikson
Editorial Adviser: Andrea Cascardi
Copy Editor: Laurie Kahn
Designer: Nathan Gassman
Page production: Picture Window Books
The illustrations in this book were rendered with watercolor.

Picture Window Books
5115 Excelsior Boulevard
Suite 232
Minneapolis, MN 55416
1-877-845-8392
www.picturewindowbooks.com

Printed in the United States of America.

Library of Congress Cataloging-in-Publication Data
Blackaby, Susan.
Steadfast tin soldier / by Hans Christian Andersen ; adapted by
Susan Blackaby ; illustrated by Charlene DeLage.
p. cm. — (Read-it! readers fairy tales)
Summary: The perilous adventure of a toy soldier who loves a
paper dancing girl culminates in tragedy for both of them.
ISBN 1-4048-0226-6
[1. Fairy tales. 2. Toys—Fiction.] I. DeLage, Charlene, 1944– ill.
II. Andersen, H. C. (Hans Christian), 1805–1875. Standhaftige
tinsoldat. English. III. Title. IV. Series.
PZ8.B5595 St 2004
[E]—dc21
                                                    2003006113

The Steadfast Tin Soldier

by Hans Christian Andersen

Adapted by Susan Blackaby
Illustrated by Charlene DeLage

Reading Advisors:
Adria F. Klein, Ph.D.
Professor Emeritus, California State University
San Bernardino, California

Kathy Baxter, M.A.
Former Coordinator of Children's Services
Anoka County (Minnesota) Library

Susan Kesselring, M.A.
Literacy Educator
Rosemount-Apple Valley-Eagan (Minnesota) School District

PiCTURE WiNDOW BOOKS
Minneapolis, Minnesota

A boy once had a set of tin soldiers.

All 25 of them were brothers.

They were made out of the same

tin spoon.

All of the soldiers were exactly alike
except the last one. He had only
one leg. But he stood as steadfast
on one leg as the others did on two.

The tin soldiers stood on a table covered with toys. The best toy was a paper castle. Wax swans swam on a glass pool in front of it.

A tiny paper dancer stood at the
castle door. She was dressed like
a princess. She wore a blue ribbon
scarf held by a tinsel rose.

The dancer kicked one leg up high behind her. The tin soldier couldn't see it. He thought she had only one leg, too.

"She is the wife for me," he thought.
"But she lives in a fine castle!
My brothers and I live in our box
like sardines
in a can."

Still, the tin soldier wanted to meet the dancer. He stretched out behind a box on the table where he could see her.

That night the toys had fun while the family slept. The chalk doodled on the slate. The nutcrackers played tag. The tin soldiers rattled their box top.

The racket woke the canary.
Tweet! Tweet! The bird sang.
In the hubbub, the tin soldier
stayed hidden. He watched
the dancer as she stood on tiptoe.

Bong! Bong! The clock chimed.
At midnight on the dot, the box
on the table flipped its lid.
Out popped Jack-in-the-box.

"Don't wish for what you can't have, soldier!" yelled Jack. The tin soldier ignored him. "Just you wait!" cried Jack.

In the morning, the boy set the tin soldier by an open window. All of a sudden, he toppled out! Did the wind blow him, or was it Jack?

The boy spent hours looking.
He didn't see the soldier stuck
between two stones. It started raining,
and the boy went inside.

17

After the storm, two boys spotted
the soldier's leg sticking up.
"Look what I found!" said one.
"He needs a boat," said the other.

The boys sent the tin
soldier down the gutter
in a paper boat.
The boat bobbed and
swirled into a dark
tunnel under a bridge.

19

"Now where am I?" wondered the tin soldier. "This must be one of Jack's tricks. I wish the dancer were here with me right now."

Just then a big rat appeared.

"Stop and pay the toll!" he snapped.

The tin soldier sailed swiftly by.

The tin soldier held his head high.
He didn't even flinch as the boat
rushed on. Water crashed
and splashed all around him.

The boat filled with water. Sadly, the soldier thought of the dancer. "Farewell, soldier, brave and true," he said to himself. "Now there's nothing to save you."

The paper boat fell apart. Dark water closed over the tin soldier's head. Then a big fish came along and swallowed him. *Gulp!*

The fish wiggled and swam.
Then he was still for a long time.
"What next?" wondered the tin
soldier. Suddenly, he saw light.

"Look!" said the cook. "The fish had a tin soldier in his tummy!" She brought the soldier to the dinner table for everyone to see.

The tin soldier was thrilled. He was
right back where he started!
There were his brothers. There was
the dancer he loved, still on tiptoe!

Then, for no reason, the boy grabbed the soldier and threw him into the fire! Jack must have made him do it!

The flames were as hot as the love
in the tin soldier's heart. He began
to melt. But still he stood tall, looking
up at the dancer.

Then a gust of wind blew the dancer into the fire. She burst into a quick flame and was gone. The soldier melted into a lump.

The next day, the cook cleaned out the fireplace. In the ashes, she found a little tin heart and a tinsel rose burned black as coal.

Levels for *Read-it!* Readers

Blue Level

Little Red Riding Hood, by Maggie Moore 1-4048-0064-6
The Goose that Laid the Golden Egg, by Mark White 1-4048-0219-3
The Three Little Pigs, by Maggie Moore 1-4048-0071-9

Yellow Level

Cinderella, by Barrie Wade 1-4048-0052-2
Goldilocks and the Three Bears, by Barrie Wade 1-4048-0057-3
Jack and the Beanstalk, by Maggie Moore 1-4048-0059-X
The Ant and the Grasshopper, by Mark White 1-4048-0217-7
The Fox and the Grapes, by Mark White 1-4048-0218-5
The Three Billy Goats Gruff, by Barrie Wade 1-4048-0070-0
The Tortoise and the Hare, by Mark White 1-4048-0215-0
The Wolf in Sheep's Clothing, by Mark White 1-4048-0220-7

Green Level

The Emperor's New Clothes, adapted by Susan Blackaby 1-4048-0224-X
The Lion and the Mouse, by Mark White 1-4048-0216-9
The Little Mermaid, adapted by Susan Blackaby 1-4048-0221-5
The Princess and the Pea, adapted by Susan Blackaby 1-4048-0223-1
The Steadfast Tin Soldier, adapted by Susan Blackaby 1-4048-0226-6
The Ugly Duckling, adapted by Susan Blackaby 1-4048-0222-3
Thumbelina, adapted by Susan Blackaby 1-4048-0225-8